I Can't Do Anything!

Published by
MAGINATION PRESS
An Educational Publishing Foundation Book
American Psychological Association
750 First Street, NE
Washington, DC 20002

For more information about our books, including a complete catalog, please write to us,
call 1-800-374-2721, or visit our website at www.apa.org/pubs/magination.

Printed by Phoenix Color Corporation, Hagerstown, MD

Library of Congress Cataloging-in-Publication Data

Robberecht, Thierry.
[Je ne peux rien faire. English]
I can't do anything! / by Thierry Robberecht ; illustrated by Annick Masson.
pages cm
"Originally published in French as Je Ne Peux Rien Faire by Mijade Publications (Belgium)."
ISBN 978-1-4338-1309-2 (hardcover : alk. paper) — ISBN 978-1-4338-1310-8 (pbk. : alk. paper)
1. Social skills in children—Juvenile literature.
2. Social interaction in children—Juvenile literature.
3. Children—Conduct of life—Juvenile literature.
I. Masson, Annick, date, illustrator. II. Title.
BF723.S62R6313 2013
155.4'182—dc23   2012043771

Manufactured in the United States of America

First printing February 2013
10 9 8 7 6 5 4 3 2 1

by Thierry Robberecht   illustrated by Annick Masson

I Can't Do Anything!

MAGINATION PRESS • WASHINGTON, DC
American Psychological Association

Chameleon sticks his tongue out.

I can't !

Monkey makes funny faces.

I have to **Smile nicely** for the picture!

Pig can snort.

When I snort,
Mom gets mad !

Snort

Squirrel eats with his fingers.

I have to mind my
table manners!

Sloth can sleep all day long.

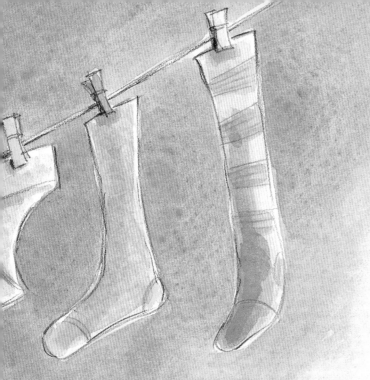

I have to wake up early to go to school.

Boar can roll in the mud.
I have to keep my new dress clean.

Hippo can have bad breath.

I have to brush my teeth
every morning
and **every evening**.

Llama spits on his friends
when he is mad.

When I spat on Leo,
I got a **time-out.**

Whale can **splish-splash** in the water.

splash!

When I splish-splashed in the bath,
Dad got angry.

Everyone loves it
when my baby brother **burps!**

burp

When I burp,
I am scolded.

I can't do anything.

I can't behave like a chameleon,

a monkey,

a pig,

a squirrel,

a sloth,

a boar,

a hippo,

a llama,

a whale,

or my brother!

I am a **perfectly well-behaved girl,** but...

I can imitate them!

Note to Parents and Other Caregivers

by Tammy L. Hughes, PhD

What parent hasn't had a child stick out his tongue at a friend, burp indiscreetly at a quiet coffee shop, or ask rather loudly why the person standing in the grocery line is so big? Like the narrator of this story, young children behave in ways that many grown-ups find impolite or discourteous. However, a child's rambunctious behavior or rude attitude isn't always intentional. Kids just may not yet realize that certain behaviors are socially unacceptable.

Despite parent requests, kids—typically between 4 and 8 years old—may be resistant to curbing that behavior and may view any modification to their actions as an imposition. Your child *will* learn socially acceptable behavior and carry that social awareness with her into young adulthood. However, if you would like to help her along, a good first step is to work as a family to set rules for social behavior and manners. Parents can also model and reward positive behaviors while reinforcing and reteaching manners and socially acceptable behavior along the way.

Set Family Rules

I Can't Do Anything! provides an opening to talk with your child about setting family rules and expectations for manners and socially acceptable behavior.

For example, you may ask your child:
- "Wouldn't it be fun to stick out such a loooong tongue?"
- "If you had a long tongue, who would you stick it out at? Why?"
- "What do you think would happen if you did that?"

A series of questions like that can segue into a conversation about alternative behavior that may be more socially acceptable, and the reasons certain manners are expected.

For example, you can ask questions such as:
- "Okay, so you can't spit at someone when you are mad. What can you do?"
- "What are some reasons people should eat with a fork and not their fingers?"
- "Can you think of any food that you would eat with your fingers? Why is it okay to eat sandwiches with your fingers but not spaghetti? Why is it okay to eat hot dogs with your fingers when they are in a bun, but not without the bun?"

However, examples of poor conduct are everywhere. Setting family rules gives your child consistent guidelines for behavior no matter where he is. For example, you may start with simple rules:
- "In our family, we don't say 'shut up.'"
- "In our house, everyone cleans up together."

Teaching your child to refer to your family rules gives her a solid foundation to use when you are not around. Further, reinforcing the use of family rules helps children feel secure in their decisions. For example:
- "You know what to do when trash is on the floor. Pick it up, right?"
- "Remind me what people should do when a friend is scared."

Explaining how and why you do things will go a long way to help your child make good decisions. For example:
- "Other people were waiting here first, so we need to get in the back of the line."
- "If someone needs to get by, let's stand to the side while we decide where we are going next."
- "Sherry is a good friend. You can be a good friend, too, when you listen to what's bothering her."

Use Positive Reinforcement

Positive reinforcement can go a long way towards learning manners and socially accepted behavior. Praise your child when he follows family rules or demonstrates social graces. For example, you can say, "You have great table manners. I'm happy you used your knife and fork at the table." Or, "I like the way you thanked the librarian for helping us find the book!" You can even give out small rewards—like a sticker—for specific behaviors.

Pick Your Battles

Not every infraction is worth fretting about. Parents and other adults should expect to teach and reteach many of the expectations they hold for their children. When your child deviates from the rules, gentle redirection may be most appropriate. For example you could say, "Yes, I agree. This pizza is way too hot to eat. When that happens, could you put the bite in your napkin instead spitting onto your plate?"

Likewise, children often need to be reminded of family rules when the context changes. For example, a child who has learned to sit quietly in the library (which she has learned through repeated practice) may not notice that a similar behavior is required during a hospital visit (when this is a new experience).

You are, in all likelihood, the best resource for teaching your child socially appropriate behavior. As children grow up and gain maturity, they begin to understand the need to act more grown up, and that it is in their best interest to behave appropriately. However, if your child's immature behavior persists, interferes with school, or negatively affects his or her social life, it may be helpful to consult a licensed psychologist or psychotherapist.

Tammy L. Hughes, PhD is a school psychologist and a professor at Duquesne University in Pittsburgh, PA.